THE
CLUTCH

GRIDIRON

THE CLUTCH

PAUL HOBLIN

darbycreek
MINNEAPOLIS

Darby Creek
A division of Lerner Publishing Group, Inc.
241 First Avenue North
Minneapolis, MN 55401 USA

For reading levels and more information, look up this title at www.lernerbooks.com.

Cover and interior images: © Pixattitude/Dreamstime.com (football player); © Eky Studio/Shutterstock.com (bolts and metal); © EFKS/Shutterstock.com (stadium background); © Kriangsak Osvapoositkul/Shutterstock.com (rust texture); © pattern line/Shutterstock.com (vintage scratched texture).

Main body text set in Janson Text LT Std 12/17.5.
Typeface provided by Adobe Systems.

Library of Congress Cataloging-in-Publication Data

Names: Hoblin, Paul, author.
Title: The clutch / Paul Hoblin.
Description: Minneapolis : Darby Creek, 2017. | Summary: "After a spectacular performance in your first, and only, high school football game, sitting on the bench might seem like a letdown. But not for this player, who is secretly scared of letting everybody down."— Provided by publisher.
Identifiers: LCCN 2016040408 (print) | LCCN 2016055329 (ebook) | ISBN 9781512439809 (lb : alk. paper) | ISBN 9781512453447 (pb : alk. paper) | ISBN 9781512448696 (eb pdf)
Subjects: | CYAC: Football—Fiction. | Self-confidence—Fiction.
Classification: LCC PZ7.H653 Cl 2017 (print) | LCC PZ7.H653 (ebook) | DDC [Fic]—dc23

LC record available at https://lccn.loc.gov/2016040408

Manufactured in the United States of America
1-42229-25778-1/5/2017

Chapter 1

The crowd's chant gets louder and louder. "STREAK!" they yell, over and over. "STREAK! STREAK! STREAK!"

I'm standing on the sideline with my Clover Ridge teammates, but I don't dare turn to look at the bleachers. Coach Cole strictly forbids fraternizing with the crowd. That's his word, *fraternizing*. I'm not exactly sure what it means. Maybe, so long as I don't talk or make eye contact with them, I *could* turn around? Even if I could, I'm not in a hurry to find out.

"STREAK! STREAK! STREAK!" the crowd continues.

It doesn't matter, anyway. I don't need to look at the crowd to know what they're chanting about.

They're chanting about me.

I'm Streak.

Or that's what they call me, anyway.

My real name is Jordan Bailey Jr. And I must be the most famous benchwarmer in the county.

To be clear, when they yell "Streak!" they're not asking me to strip off my clothes and run across the football field.

They're asking me to jog confidently to the huddle, tell one of the receivers to go deep, take the snap, and heave the ball as far as I can throw it.

That's what I did last year: chucked a perfect spiral that remained airborne for sixty yards. Or was it seventy? Or eighty? The pass gets longer every time Lance Brockman talks about it. He's the one who caught the pass for a touchdown. He also happens to be my best friend. A few days later, he quit the team to defend my honor. (Long story.) That's why he's in the stands now, chanting on my behalf. (That's a long story too.)

Not that his chanting has ever done any good. Other than that one play last season, I haven't taken a single snap. Almost my whole high school football career has been spent on the sideline, watching Curt Cole, the coach's son, crouch under center.

"STREAK! STREAK! STREAK!"

My guess? Lance isn't even watching the game right now. Instead of facing the field, he's probably facing the crowd, getting them riled up, waving his arms like a conductor.

"STREAK! STREAK! STREAK!"

For the first time in a year, Lance and the crowd might get what they want. Our defense just intercepted a pass and took it to the house.

I look at the scoreboard: Clover Ridge 17, Iron Lake 3.

That we're winning isn't surprising. We're one of the best teams in the state. More accurately, we have one of the best defenses in the state. Our offense? Not so much. I'd say we're mediocre, and that's being kind.

Lance would say we're an embarrassment. No, not we—Curt. He's the embarrassment, according to Lance. Total rag arm. The result is that we win almost every game, but not by much.

"STREAK! STREAK! STREAK!"

This time, though, we're up by two touchdowns, and there's less than three minutes to play.

It's impossible to imagine Iron Lake scoring once, let alone twice. They've hardly gained a yard the entire second half.

"STREAK! STREAK! STREAK!"

My gaze is fixed on the field, but out of the corner of my eye, I'm pretty sure I see Coach Cole shuffling in my direction. Is he finally going to tell me to warm up? Is he actually going to put me in for the last series before the clock expires?

That's when the impossible happens. The Iron Lake quarterback throws a pass that could easily be picked off by two of our guys. Instead, they run into each other. The pass bounces off one of their helmets and lands in the intended receiver's hands. Fifty-two yards later, it's a 17–10 ball game.

The crowd is still yelling, "STREAK!"— but Coach Cole ignores them. He sends his son back onto the field to run out the clock.

For the first time ever, the chants become boos.

Loud ones.

I turn around without thinking.

Lance's face is red from anger, and he's not alone. The crowd is unhappy. Their hands are cupped around their mouths so their voices will carry as far as possible.

"BOOOOO!"

Clover Ridge is about to win its sixth straight home game, but our fans don't seem to care. They want to see me play, and they won't be happy until they get what they want.

In fact, there might only be one person in the whole stadium who *is* happy right now.

Me.

I may be too much of a coward to say it out loud, but the truth is that I never want to play football again.

Chapter 2

I sit on a bench in the locker room and wait for my teammates to leave.

Well, all of my teammates except one.

As usual, Curt is the last to leave.

For one thing, Coach Cole is his ride.

For another, he doesn't seem to have anywhere to go except home. No, correction— he doesn't seem to *want* to go anywhere else. When I first joined the team last year, I remember him getting invited to parties or to just hang out with the rest of the guys. He would shrug his shoulders and say he needed to get his rest. By the way he said it, it sounded like he was telling the rest of us that we should get our rest too. He sounded, in other words, like his dad. It didn't take long for our teammates to stop inviting him anywhere—both because they knew what his answer would be and because they were afraid he'd nark on them to Coach.

"Hey, Curt?" I say to him now.

He's sitting like he always does—his big shoulders hunched.

He lifts his eyes an inch or two, just enough to see me, but he doesn't say anything. Curt's never been much of a talker.

"Just wanted to say good game, man," I tell him.

This is what I've been waiting around to tell him. Thanks to Lance and all the chanting, I bet it's been a long time since someone congratulated Curt for yet another win.

Curt doesn't respond right away. He just looks around at the empty locker room.

"Don't worry," he says finally, still not looking at me. "I won't tell Lance you said so."

He gets up, his big shoulders knocking into me as he heads to Coach's office.

Sometimes he makes it really difficult to feel sorry for him. I know Lance gives the guy a hard time, but I really did mean it when I congratulated him.

***

The house is dark when I open the front door.

"How'd it go?" Mom says over her shoulder.

The only light in the room is coming from the glowing TV screen. Mom is in front of it. On the couch, watching a baseball game on mute. It's October—baseball play-off time. For the next month my mom's eyes will be glued to the TV.

"Fine," I say. "We won."

"You mean the players who got a chance to play won," she says, still staring at the screen.

If it's harsh, she doesn't mean it to be. She's actually trying to be sympathetic. She's sad and angry that I'm not getting a chance to really be a part of a team.

My bench warming is personal for her, and not only because I'm her son. She doesn't just feel sorry for me; she feels sorry for her own athletic career. Mom was a star softball player growing up. She led her conference in batting average and RBIs for three straight years. Which is why, as a senior, she decided to switch over to the boys' baseball team. She has always said she wanted a different challenge; she wanted to play the game she grew up watching on TV. The good news was that she made the team. Or at least she thought it was good news at the time. Looking back, she says the only reason the coach didn't cut her was because of the media frenzy it would cause. This was over twenty years ago, so my mom's decision to try out for a boys' team was a big deal. At least one story had been written about her in a national newspaper. Still, it turned out the coach had no intention of letting her play in a game— probably because that too would have caused a stir. After being called a traitor and even worse for leaving the girls' team, my mom spent the entire season sitting in the dugout.

"Actually," I say, "I almost *did* get to play today."

Mom turns away from the TV screen. "Really?"

"Really."

I try to make my voice sound as excited as hers.

"Don't leave me hanging," she says eagerly.

The living room light goes on.

My dad, his eyelids heavy from sleep, stands by the switch. "Sorry, gang," he says groggily. "Don't mean to be a buzzkill, but can you try to keep your voices down? I have early-morning rounds."

Dad's an emergency room doctor, so when he says *early* he means it.

"Sorry, babe," Mom says.

"Yeah. Sorry, Dad."

He yawns and says, "You should get some rest too, Jordan."

"I will," we say in unison.

It's a long-running joke we all make because both of us—Mom and me—are named Jordan. That's right. I was named after my mother. Thus the Jordan Bailey *Jr*. My mom's the *Sr*. When I was a kid I thought that was weird, especially since all my friends said so. And even more especially since my parents didn't. After all, Mom and Dad explained, Jordan was both a girl's and a boy's name, right? That part actually made sense to me, and after they met her, kids stopped teasing me about being named after my mom.

Growing up, I thought my dad was a nice guy, but it was my mom who was more fun to hang out with. She's an elementary school gym teacher, so she always had ideas and equipment for some sport we could play.

Frankly, I wanted to be just like her. For most adults, going to work meant doing something super serious and boring. But for Mom it meant playing games. Even now, Mom is staying up late watching baseball while Dad is standing half asleep by the light switch.

He says goodnight and turns the lights back off as Mom turns to me.

"Tell me everything," she whispers.

And I do. I tell her about the chanting, and

about seeing Coach Cole headed my way. I tell her about the interception, and about the crowd booing.

"You're going to get your chance," she says, trying but failing to whisper.

I haven't heard her sound this hopeful in a while.

I let her believe that I'm as hopeful as she is. I let her believe that Jordan Bailey might finally get to play.

Chapter 3

Once again, I hear the chant: "STREAK! STREAK! STREAK!"

The difference is that I'm not at a football game. I'm at school.

Lunch, more specifically.

A minute ago, I stepped into the cafeteria. As soon as Lance saw me, he glanced over at Curt, and I knew that what was going to happen next wasn't going to be good. He looked around the table and started chanting. What began as a few of the football players soon spread across the cafeteria. Now most of the students are chanting.

I make my way through the crazed crowd to the long table where all the football players eat. By this point, Lance is standing on top of the table, leading the cheers. He waves his arms and starts yelling "STREAK!" again. Instantly everyone joins in.

"What are you doing?" I yell, staring up at him. He's six and a half feet tall and all muscle just standing on the floor. He looks like a giant standing on the table like this.

"What?" he says, his arms still waving to the beat of the chant.

"Is this really necessary?" I ask him.

I think he must have understood me because he quiets the crowd by lowering his arms.

"Streak speaks!" he says.

I don't get it, but a lot of other people do.

"SPEECH! SPEECH! SPEECH!" they chant.

Before I know what's happening, Lance crouches down, grabs under my armpits, and lifts me onto the table with him.

He signals to the crowd, and the cafeteria goes quiet. I look out at all the students. They look back at me. Even the students that weren't cheering before are listening now. It seems that they are all interested in what is going to happen next. What "the great Streak" is going to say. I look around at them, trying to find just one face that isn't staring back at me—one person who's sitting there, eating their lunch and minding their business.

And then I do find someone who is definitely ignoring the commotion.

He's at the end of the table I'm standing on.

Curt Cole's bulky body is hunched over his tray. He's either pretending not to hear the chants or protecting himself from them like he protects the football during a quarterback sneak.

Lance elbows me in the ribs. "They're waiting, man," he says under his breath.

All of the sudden I'm even more flustered. No, not just flustered. Mad.

What does Lance want me to say?

Lance elbows me again.

"Ummm. Thanks," I finally say. "Enjoy your lunches."

There's more silence. Apparently I'm supposed to say more. But I can't think of anything.

Lance grabs my right arm and lifts it into the air. "I guess when you have a golden arm like this, you don't need to say many words!"

The crowd erupts in more cheers as I scramble off the table, still fuming. If Lance doesn't get off the table, I tell myself, I'll pull him down.

Luckily for him, he *does* get off the table. In fact, he jumps off it . . . and over one of our teammates. A couple of the guys high-five Lance as he slides into his seat next to me.

I wait for everyone to turn back to their food before I punch Lance in the arm.

"Hey, what the . . . ?" he says, rubbing his arm.

"What are you doing?" I demand.

"What are you talking about, dude? I'm fighting the good fight, just like I always do."

"Do you have to do it in front of Curt?" I say under my breath.

I mean, the guy's just trying to eat his lunch.

"It's in front of Curt at the games too," Lance points out, not at all under his breath. "The dude sucks."

"Keep your voice down," I tell him. "You're practically shouting. Curt's like eight feet from us."

"Good. I hope he hears me. Maybe he'll finally do the honorable thing and fall on his sword."

"Fall on his sword?"

"Quit, dude. Or at least hand over the starting job to you."

"That's why you're being such a jerk? Because you think it will convince Curt to step aside?"

"Well," he says, finally lowering his volume, "that and because I need to get the guys riled up for all of the cameras at practice this afternoon."

"What do you mean, the cameras at practice?" I practically choke on the words.

"Some dude from the news is coming. Somehow they found out about all the chanting and booing last night and—"

"Somehow?" I interrupt.

Lance shrugs his hulking shoulders and raises his eyebrows. "I may have sent in an anonymous call," he says. "Local town fights for quarterback justice, etcetera, etcetera."

"And they bought that?"

"Who wouldn't? How often does the home team get booed while winning?"

He says this with pride, like he's really accomplished something, which makes me even angrier. But it also leaves me a little in awe. Lance might be a jerk, but he's also the best hype man I've ever known.

"Anyway," he continues, voice lowered confidentially, "the anonymous caller told them to find me to get the scoop. I told them to meet me at the field."

"Is that even allowed?" I say. "Are they allowed on school property?"

Lance shrugs his shoulders again. "I'm sure they'll figure it out." He claps me on the shoulder. "You know how the principal loves publicity. And as long as they're looking for a story, I might as well make you the star you're meant to be."

Chapter 4

It was Lance who convinced me to join the team last year.

School hadn't started yet, but football practice had. The team had a new coach. Back then, Lance didn't have much to say about him. It was the quarterback he was worried about.

We were tossing the football around in my backyard after Lance's first couple of practices as he complained about the team. "This Curt kid," he told me, "is a joke. When I first saw him I was pretty impressed. Short but stocky. Sturdy. I thought he would be a good replacement for the QB that graduated last year. Then I saw him throw. At first I thought he was kidding. A guy that bulky's gotta be able to put more on the ball than that, right? Nope. That's when I found out his last name and put two and two together. Coach Cole is his old man. Seriously, dude, we need you to join."

"I'm not even that good, Lance. Besides," I said, "there's no point in me joining the team if this Curt kid is the coach's son. Even if *my* dad would ever let me." I tossed the football back to Lance. "Why would the coach bench his own son?"

"Are you kidding me, you've dominated in our flag league this summer. You clearly have a better arm than Curt. Besides, Coach Cole wants to win, doesn't he?" Lance winked. "Plus, he doesn't want his star player unhappy." Based on the way he was pointing at his own flexed bicep, it was pretty clear he was talking about himself.

He was cocky, but he wasn't wrong. He'd been all-conference last year as a freshman, and had only gotten bigger and faster since then. Division I schools had already sent him recruitment letters. All a quarterback had to do was throw the ball in his general direction and good things usually happened. (This is one of the reasons people listen to him, I think. For some reason people care more about what good athletes have to say than regular people.)

I snorted at his muscle-man pose. "Sometimes you really are too much to take in. Besides, like I said, you don't have to convince me to join the team. You have to convince my dad."

I'd been trying to get my dad to let me play in the tackle leagues since fifth grade, but nothing I said changed what he called the "medical realities of the situation." Sometimes it seems like my dad can't quite shut down the doctor part of his brain. "The cranial science is devastating and undeniable," he liked to say. This was his fancy way of saying he was worried I'd get a concussion.

"Easy," Lance said, tossing the ball back. "I'll explain that life is fleeting. That we have to take hold of the moment and not let go."

"And you think that'll work?" I asked. My dad didn't usually fall for greeting-card sentiments.

"Of course it'll work, dude. Adults are total suckers for sob stories. Especially when you're literally sobbing."

"You're going to cry?"

"Sure," Lance said.

Right then and there, in the middle of our game of catch, Lance started weeping. His breathing became shallow and thick. Actual tears trickled and then gushed down his cheeks.

"Wow," I said. I'd heard of people who could cry on command, but this was next-level acting. It was the first time I realized how incredible Lance was at playing on people's emotions.

He winked at me again, the tears instantly stopping. "But more importantly, *you're* going to cry," he told me.

I stood there stunned for a minute as Lance walked over. Finally, I mustered up a response to Lance's performance. "I don't know how to do that, Lance. Cry just 'cause."

Without any warning, Lance pinched my forearm and yanked out several hairs. My eyes became watery from both pain and surprise.

"Perfect," Lance said. "Now you're ready to help me talk to your dad."

I nodded, my sight still blurry.

"This fall, dude," he said. "You and me. Nothing's gonna stop us."

***

It turned out Lance was right about my dad. He caved when he saw the waterworks.

Coach Cole, on the other hand?

Not even the loss of his star player was going to change his mind.

Chapter 5

When I started playing for the high school team, Lance had big dreams for us.

It's safe to say the season didn't go as planned.

The first thing Lance did was bring me into Coach Cole's office.

"Hey, Coach," Lance said. "Thought you should meet our new quarterback. The two of us have been tearing up the summer league together and I don't see any reason to stop now."

Coach Cole's back was to us. We waited for him to swivel in his chair, but he didn't. He didn't even take his eyes away from the game footage he was watching on his TV screen.

"Coach," Lance tried again, this time talking louder. "This is—"

"Jason's the equipment manager," Coach Cole interrupted. "He can get you suited up. Do me a favor and tell any other new guys the same thing. I'm busy."

We stood there a few moments longer, waiting for him to turn around and look at us.

He didn't.

***

"Don't sweat it," Lance said after that first meeting.

Still, I could tell he was shaken. And angry. He'd made a couple of spectacular plays in his freshman season, including a one-handed, sprawling, above-the-helmet grab that was featured on ESPN.

A lot of people were impressed with him, and I think he assumed our new coach would be one of them. Instead, Coach had barely acknowledged his presence.

"Once he sees you sling a few passes," Lance reassured me, "he'll have to take notice."

One problem. There was no reason for Coach Cole to see me throw any passes. Despite what Lance had said about me in his office, Coach didn't treat me as an up-and-coming star. He treated me as a nobody.

I'd assumed there would be a competition for the quarterback job. But as far as Coach was concerned, the decision had already been made.

Curt, his son, was also his QB.

That's the way it was for the first game of the season, and the second, and the third.

I was disappointed, but Lance? The kid was furious.

So furious that he stopped running his routes. "I'm not just a decoy. Besides," he said, "It's not like the other team really believes Curt can throw the ball to me. What's the point of me running hard? Everyone knows the dude's just going to tuck the ball under his armpit and run for a couple yards. That's all he can do, so that's all he will do."

He'd complain to me, loudly, as I stood on the sideline. We were required to keep our helmets on, but Lance ignored that rule.

His helmetless yelling made me uncomfortable even then. It definitely didn't seem like the best way to get on the coach's good side. More than once I was pretty sure I saw Coach look our way and glare at him—or maybe at both of us.

But I also felt sorry for Lance. And for me.

Because what he was saying wasn't wrong. As far as I could tell, Curt really did have a rag arm. And Lance really was suffering the consequences. We rarely threw the ball anymore. When we did, it was a screen or something in the flats. Nothing downfield. Lance never got to run or catch the ball like he had done the previous season. He really *was* just a decoy.

***

It wasn't until an away game against St. Augustine when we were way up that Coach called me over.

"Bailey!" he barked. "You know how to take a snap?"

I was insulted, even though it was a totally valid question. After all, the only football I'd ever played was flag, so I'd only gotten the ball from the shotgun. Then again, the reason he didn't know whether I could stand under center was because he'd never given me a chance during practice.

The honest answer was that I wasn't sure whether I knew how to take a snap or not. But I wasn't about to admit that. I wanted to get in the game, so there was only one answer to his question.

"Yes, sir," I said.

"Load right, forty-four dive left on two," Coach barked in the earhole of my helmet. Then he pushed me onto the field.

Anyway, that's what I think he said.

In retrospect.

At the time, my adrenaline was out of control. My heart was pounding in my ears. And the truth is that I wasn't one hundred percent sure what he said.

Not that it would have mattered, because I hadn't memorized the playbook yet.

As I trotted out to the huddle, I tried to recall his words. But my brain had gone numb. So had my legs. I couldn't feel my cleats digging into the grass, or my knee drop to the ground as I joined the huddle. It was too loud. Was it the noise from the crowd or was it from my thoughts scrambling every which way at a million miles an hour? My tongue, too, had become heavy and numb. Even if I could have thought of a play to call, I don't think I could have pronounced the words.

"Streak?"

The voice cut through the noise. I knew who it belonged to.

I nodded to Lance, who was grinning wildly. The others must have felt I was nodding at them, too, because they left the huddle to get in their positions.

And just like that I was crouched under center, taking the first and only snap of my high school career.

Chapter 6

What happened next, according to Lance, was the play of his dreams.

He watched the center snap the ball and took off like a sprinter after a gun shot.

He raced down the field, his legs a blur.

It wasn't until he'd left both the cornerback and the free safety in his dust that he turned his head.

He looked over his shoulder into the black sky

There was the football, spiraling perfectly. Just beginning its descent.

He'd been running for thirty, forty, fifty

yards, and he wasn't done yet.

He didn't catch up to the ball until he was in the back of the end zone.

It was a thing of beauty, according to Lance.

Poetry in motion, he said.

Chapter

7

Here's what happened after the snap, according to me.

I bobbled the ball.

Stumbling backward, I looked down. The football wobbled as I trapped it against my hip.

Finally, I got a better grip and lifted my eyes.

I wanted to find Lance, see if he was open.

But I didn't find him.

It wasn't just his legs that were a blur. It was everything.

For one thing, I wasn't used to looking at the field through a helmet and facemask. All I could make out were bodies and limbs lunging and lurching at me.

For a sophomore I was already fairly tall—a shade over six feet—but the players around me seemed taller.

Adrenaline gushed through me, swamping my brain.

I couldn't think straight, so my body took over decision-making duties.

It sensed the proximity of violence. It knew that this violence was closing in.

I was in fight-or-flight mode.

Except this was football, so there was no actual fight. And there was nowhere to run.

The only thing I could do, my body decided, was throw.

No, not throw. *Heave.*

It sounds like the pass itself was indeed a beauty. That I'd somehow managed to perfectly calculate Lance's speed and the exact yardage of the field. That my throw was a testament to our chemistry, his speed, and my throwing talent. But that's not how it felt.

It felt like pure luck.

And then it felt painful.

The truth is that I never saw the football in the air. While Lance and almost everyone else in the stadium watched the ball soar through the night, someone's shoulder pad rammed into my stomach, snapping my head back. Somebody else's helmet speared me in the back. As my throw made a poetic arc that cut through the glare of the stadium's lights, I fell hard and then lie on the field trying to get my breath back.

A teammate eventually reached out a hand to help me up. By then, though, I wasn't sure I ever wanted to get up again. All my life I'd played video game football, and watched real football on TV and YouTube videos of body-crunching tackles. I *rooted* for these collisions on the field, the bigger the better. But I'd never experienced one myself. I'd never experienced what it was like to listen to people celebrate while you're having trouble breathing. If no one was concerned about me, this play must have been common. It seemed like somebody should be running for the stretcher. Calling the ambulance. Instead, no one seemed to care about me at all. This pain, I realized, must be something I should expect on every play.

I shuffled off the field, back to the sidelines.

Chapter

8

Lance has been telling his version of that play every chance he gets. He explains, over and over, how Coach yelled at me for not doing the boring play he told me to do. He says, to whoever will listen, that I was benched for proving how talented I was.

"That's why I quit," he repeats all the time. "To support Jordan. What Coach did to him was unfair, and I wasn't about to stand for it."

Meanwhile, I haven't told *anyone* my version of events.

I haven't admitted that after that play I was terrified to ever step on a football field again.

I haven't confessed that I still am terrified.

I don't know why, exactly, I've kept my feelings to myself. At first I think I liked all the praise. Random students were suddenly noticing me. Guys would clap me on the shoulder. Girls would tell me how sorry they were that the coach wouldn't let me play.

Besides, how was I supposed to tell the people who truly cared about me?

If I told my mom that it was a lucky play, that I was relieved I didn't have to play, she'd be crushed.

If I told my dad how sore my ribs and back were, he'd say he was right all along that football was too dangerous. He might even insist I quit the team. Back then, I wasn't sure I really wanted to quit. I thought I might just be in shock. After all, I'd never been hit so hard before. Maybe I'd get over it and want to keep playing.

I never even told Lance. That's what I feel worst about. The guy quit the team for *me*. It didn't take me long to feel guilty about that, but it was already too late. He'd already burned every possible bridge with Coach. He'd begun chanting my name in the crowd. He'd ripped on Coach's kid for all to hear. There was no way Coach Cole was ever going to let him back onto the team. And even if he did, there was no way Lance could accept. He had way too much pride for that.

So Lance kept telling his version. And I kept not telling mine.

And now Lance was going to tell his version in front of cameras.

All this time I've known what I *should* say to others, if I wasn't such a coward. I've known that my story would make all this nonsense go away.

But now the nonsense has gotten too big. I'm afraid there's nothing I can say or do to stop it.

Chapter 9

When I arrive at practice, I see a news truck parked on the street. The camera guy and reporter are standing next to the fence too.

My best guess? They already got permission from the school to film, but Coach won't allow them on the field. This is as close as they're going to get.

But it's close enough. Especially since Lance is standing with them. The reporter holds the microphone to his face. Lance is pointing right at me. So is the camera.

I put on my helmet and pretend not to notice them.

When I get home after practice, there's Lance again. Or his face, anyway.

He's on TV.

"All I'm saying is Jordan can throw the ball sixty, seventy yards," he says. "But Coach doesn't even let him throw passes in practice. He is a huge asset to the team, but he is being completely ignored."

The news program goes back to the studio, where the reporter I saw at practice sits with two news anchors. "I couldn't get any video evidence of Jordan's throwing ability," she says, "because the young man I talked to was right. Coach Able Cole didn't let him pass. Most of the students I talked to were in agreement, though. This Jordan Bailey has quite the arm."

The news anchors show one last shot of me standing at practice then turn to a story about gluten.

The TV turns off.

"Is that true?"

It's my mom's voice, and it's coming from the kitchen.

I take a whiff of whatever's baking in the oven. Smells like Mom's specialty: frozen meals. Beef with gravy this time, I'm guessing.

"The coach won't even let you throw during practice?" she asks. She has a pot holder in one hand and the remote in the other.

"Sort of," I tell her.

The truth is that it's more complicated than that. For one thing, I am the *backup* quarterback, so it seems logical to me that I don't get as many snaps as Curt does. And even Curt doesn't throw on Mondays. Our team spends Mondays focusing on defense and our running game. It's been this way since I joined the team. Lance knows this; he was on the team too, after all. It's no doubt why he wanted the reporters to come to practice today. He knew it would play right into my story. He set it up to make it look like Coach wouldn't let me throw.

I'm going to tell Mom all of this, but she interrupts me.

"I'd be happy to run some routes for you after dinner," she says.

She stands there in her regular getup: a hooded sweatshirt, warm-up pants, and sneakers.

"Sure, Mom," I tell her. "That'd be great."

She smiles. "First, though, we'll feast on meat that tastes like cardboard."

She turns to the oven, then looks back.

"Hey, Jordan," she says.

"Yes, Jordan?" I respond.

She smiles again, but she falters and the smile fades. "I'm really sorry you have to go through this nonsense. Maybe tomorrow things will get better. You know, after this news report."

I seriously doubt it. I'm not even sure I know what *better* would look like.

"Maybe," I say.

Chapter 10

The next afternoon I lace up my cleats in the locker room.

"Bailey!" a voice booms through the locker bank.

"Yes, sir?" I say.

"My office," Coach shouts.

"Yes, sir."

I follow him to his office. He grunts to the chair on the other side of his desk.

I sit.

We sit there in silence. As usual, his face is red and sweaty. We haven't even started practice but sweat drips off the brim of his cap.

It darkens the gray tufts of hair by his ears. His sharp cheekbones are scarlet. It's as if his blood really is boiling. Half of me expects the sweat drops to sizzle when they land on his desk.

"You're going to take a few more snaps than usual this week," he says.

"Really?" I say. The comment catches me so off guard I can't help also blurting: "Why?"

Coach sighs. "Because I'm tired of this," he says. On cue, the blood drains from his cheeks and then the rest of his face. I honestly didn't know Coach was capable of being tired. "The only game I've ever liked to play is football," he says. "But if your friend insists on playing the media game, I guess I'll play too." He shakes his head. "We're undefeated and our fans are booing. You ever heard of such a thing?"

I don't answer because I'm pretty sure I'm not supposed to. He's staring at the ceiling as he talks, still shaking his head.

Another sigh.

"So fine," he says. "I'll play along. I'll talk to the media. Tell them you're getting just as many snaps in practice as Curt. When they bring their cameras, they'll see that's the truth. They'll report that you have just as good a chance of starting on Friday as Curt. How's that sound to you?"

I don't answer because I have no idea what to say. I'm stunned. I feel like I can't move my body, my tongue, my mouth.

"That's what I thought," Coach says. "That's what I've thought all along. I've been doing this a long time, son. I know a scared kid when I see one. You might have others fooled, but not me. You don't want to have anything to do with football, do you?"

Is this another rhetorical question? Is he going to make me say it?

"Every time I look your way, you are hiding in a crowd of players. If I meet your eyes, you looked away. You've never acted like someone who wants the bright lights on them. I just have one more question, son. If you don't want to play, why are you still on the team? Why didn't you do the honorable thing and quit. It sure would have saved us a lot of grief."

This is the second time in less than two days someone has described quitting as the honorable thing. Lance was talking about Curt, but Coach is right. *I'm* the one who should have quit.

"Forget it," Coach says. "I'm not about to tell a kid who shows up for practice every day and keeps his mouth shut that he has to quit. Not you. Not my son, even though—believe me—I'd understand if he did want to quit." The blood is boiling in Coach's face again, but he lets out another sigh. "Maybe you could have prevented all this nonsense, but that doesn't make it your fault."

"Thanks," I say. I'm not sure he hears me, though, because I'm practically whispering. I'm surprised by how good it feels to have someone say this isn't my fault, whether or not I believe him.

"So," Coach says, "we'll play the media game this week. We'll pretend you have a chance to start on Friday. But between you and me, as long as Curt is able to stand, you're never going to get on the field again."

I'm almost positive I don't say thanks again—not out loud—but maybe I do.

Because Coach says, "You're welcome" as I walk out the door.

Chapter 11

As expected, the camera, the reporter, and Lance are all by the field again at practice.

"Streak! Hey, Bailey!"

Lance waves me over.

"They want an interview with the would-be star!" he yells.

I don't move. I stand there trying to come up with an excuse to not have to go over there.

Luckily, someone blows a whistle to get practice started. Was it Coach Cole? Was he helping me get out of this interview? Maybe. Then again, it could have just as easily been one of his assistant coaches. Either way, I'm grateful.

I shrug my shoulders in apology to Lance and the camera crew, then jog toward the field with my teammates.

"The humble superstar," I hear Lance explain to the camera. "They're rare these days. It's sort of refreshing, you know? But it's also sad. The last thing Jordan wants to do is cause a fuss. That's why I'm speaking up on his behalf."

***

Coach keeps his word about giving me more snaps in practice.

Right from the get-go, Curt and I take turns playing with the first team. We go through all our running plays and then go through them again.

Then it's time to go through our pass plays.

By now I'm feeling better about football than I have in a long time. I've got a good sweat going. Tuesdays are no-contact practices, so I don't need to worry about getting crushed when I drop back to pass.

I take the snap and survey the field. The first thing I look for is the receiver running a post pattern. That's a deep route. If he's not open, then I'm supposed to check down for the receivers running shorter routes.

But the receiver downfield *is* open.

Barely.

He's got half a step on the cornerback. To complete the pass, I'm going to have to lead him perfectly and put some zip on the ball.

I do both.

It's been a long time since I planted my foot in the ground and really let the football fly. It feels great. I watch the ball race through the air, spiraling clockwise.

My pass hits the receiver right in the chest.

Literally.

He doesn't get his hands up fast enough, and the football bounces off the front of his shoulder and drops to the ground. Maybe I threw the ball too fast for him? Maybe he's not used to needing to have his hands ready so quickly? Maybe he didn't even realize he was open? It's safe to say that Curt would never have attempted a difficult throw like that. It's also safe to say that our receiver is not very good.

"Did you see that pass?"

Lance's voice startles me out of my thoughts.

"This guy could throw a ball through a tire from forty yards out in a windstorm!" Lance says.

He's not the only one who's calling attention to my throw. The camera is aimed right at me. Teammates smile through their facemasks and clap me on the shoulder.

"I'm telling you," Lance shouts excitedly, "if Coach Cole just gave him a shot, he could make throws like that all day."

He's over a hundred yards away, still on the other side of the fence, but I can hear him crystal clear.

I had completely forgotten about Lance and the camera. Until now. And now that I remember, I can't seem to think about anything else. Even as we line up for another play, all I can think about is the camera. If I screw up, they'll see me. If I play well, it'll be harder for Coach to start Curt, not me.

The center snaps me the ball, but when I drop back, my mind seems to go blank. I see the receiver hustling up the sideline, but I can sense the camera on me. If I throw the ball deep, really deep, and if I throw the ball relatively on target, Lance will ooh and ahh over my incredible arm.

If I check down to the running back in the flats, Lance will praise my decision-making skills.

But I don't do either. I mean, I do throw it deep—just not deep enough. I watch my pass float a pathetic twenty-five yards and then plop to the ground like a duck shot out of the air.

There's silence.

Silence that Lance tries his best to fill.

"Hey, man, no worries. You're a little rusty. Who wouldn't be?" he yells to me before turning back to the reporters. "Keep the tape rolling, man. The next throw's guaranteed to take your breath away."

What if it doesn't? I think. But then I realize I know the answer: they will go away. No more cameras. No more news stories. Maybe this could work to my advantage.

It takes me a little while to really focus back on throwing the ball, but even when I do they aren't all great passes. I make sure of it.

When two receivers run crossing patterns I don't take aim at all before letting go of the ball. I overthrow them so badly it isn't clear which of them is my target. My next pass is easily intercepted.

Not all my throws are terrible. Sometimes I do let the ball rip with ease. But every once in a while, I botch a pass pretty bad. Sometimes because I blank under the pressure, and sometimes because I don't try. Every time the ball falls to the ground or is picked off by one of the defenders, I secretly have hopes that if I screw up enough, the cameras will disappear.

My teammates become more deflated with each throw. I don't blame them. I feel the same way.

I wish I could spend the practice cutting loose on every play, throwing the ball the way I'm capable of doing and seeing what happens. And then, at the end of practice, I wish I could shake Curt's hand and wish him good luck at the next game.

I wish the camera would go away. Lance too.

Chapter 12

It's weird seeing Coach on TV. His face looks too big. It's as red as usual but looks less intense. His voice isn't as gruff. In fact, it's barely audible.

He may not look angry, but my guess is that he's furious. The reason he's talking under his breath is to keep his frustration at bay. He can't believe he has to answer these questions, all because of a player (me) who he knows doesn't even want to play.

Mom turns the volume up, but it doesn't help much. He's still basically mumbling.

His words come in and out: " . . . decided to give Bailey a closer look . . . Team first, individuals second . . . We're trying to focus on the game ahead of us . . . Like I said, the kid's going to get a shot, okay?"

The screen switches back to the studio. The reporter continues to sum up the interview with Coach. Her voice blares. Rather than turning the volume back to a reasonable volume, Mom turns off the TV.

Apparently she'd rather get the report from me.

"Is it true?" she asks. "Is he finally giving you a fair shot?"

I don't want to lie to Mom again—I've done enough of that already. But I also don't want to explain my meeting with Coach before practice, or the way I played during practice.

So I say, "I got half the snaps at practice today."

It's true, even if it's not quite what she asked.

"In that case, I'll see you on Friday," Mom says.

"You're coming to the game?"

She hardly ever goes to my games because she says it's too painful to see me standing there on the sidelines being ignored by the coach.

"Are you kidding me?" she says. "Of course I'll be there."

"It's away. At North Valley."

"I wouldn't miss it, Jordan. If you're playing I'll be there."

"The thing is," I say, "I didn't throw very well today. I mean, there's still a good chance I won't play on Friday."

Mom springs up from the couch. "Only one way to fix that," she says. She heads to the closet and comes back with car keys in one hand and a football in the other. "You tell me the routes and I'll run them," she says, flipping the football to me.

We head for the car.

"Hey, Mom?" I turn to her.

"Yes, Jordan?" she says.

"Do you think Dad will be able to come on Friday?"

"You know he doesn't like to watch." Then,

with a sympathetic smile, Mom adds "We'll ask him tonight, okay? He should be back from the hospital by the time we're done practicing." She smiles bigger. "Otherwise," she says, "it's another TV dinner for us."

Chapter 13

Curt starts at quarterback on Friday because of course he does. Coach Cole made it perfectly clear in his office. I have no chance of starting, no matter what he tells the reporter or even the team.

I know this, even if no one else does.

What I *am* surprised about is the lack of booing as we enter the stadium.

Granted, this is an away game. But enough of our fans showed up to make their voices heard.

And there *are* a few jeers from the crowd. But the overall spirit is dampened by the thick rain pelting the fans, and now the players, in the face.

It's falling from the sky in torrents. Thick, heavy, constant.

The rain drenches through my uniform in minutes. It whips across my face. I have to reach through my facemask to wipe my eyes as I stand on the sidelines.

Maybe that's why Curt doesn't have to deal with the fans' wrath. They're too busy wiping their own soaked faces.

Besides, by the time Curt has run the first few plays, they have to admit he's playing really well.

This isn't exactly passing weather. Both the ball and the field are too slippery. Water bubbles through the grass with every step. By the second quarter, there's no grass left. Just mud.

Running backs slip and fumble the football. Linebackers attempt to recover the fumble and fumble it themselves.

The only one who's not slipping and fumbling is Curt. His sturdy legs anchor him to the ground. He plants and cuts through the mucky field, gaining huge chunks of yards. While everyone else slips and sprawls face-first or falls on their butts, Curt churns through the mud without slowing or sliding.

At the half, we're beating North Valley by four touchdowns. One of them was a fumble recovery. Curt scored the other three.

Because it's an away game, we're wearing our white jerseys. But as the game winds down, only Curt's jersey is still (relatively) white. The rest of the players' uniforms are coated in brown slime.

There are only a few minutes left.

The score: 38–0.

The game, clearly, is all but over.

But Curt isn't letting up. He scampers up the field for twelve yards. On the next play he cuts across the fifty, the forty-five, the forty.

Fifty-eight seconds left.

It's first and ten on North Valley's thirty-eight yard line. All Curt has to do is take a knee and the game is over. But Curt keeps on playing. He runs an option play. He could pitch the ball to the running back, but he doesn't do that either.

He tucks the ball under his arm and turns up the field.

Or he tries to.

For the first time all day, he slips.

No, that's not quite right.

He doesn't slip. He sticks.

His foot gets stuck in the mud. As a result, his leg bends one way, his body the other.

No, he doesn't slip. He crumbles.

As the refs blow their whistles and players get up and shuffle back to their sides, Curt's body is still lying motionless in the muck.

More whistles.

Coach Cole hustles across the field toward his quarterback. His son.

The trainer follows him.

There are a few moments where no one seems to know what to do. Coach and the trainer are talking, but I can't hear what they're saying. Finally, James and Lando, two of our offensive linemen, hoist Curt to his feet.

Taking short, careful steps, the two linemen help Curt off the field. Curt hops on his right foot; the other one dangles weirdly.

That's when I look at his grimacing face. He's usually so closed off, but right now his face is full of emotion. Pain. Frustration. Anger. Defeat. They're all on full display.

I watch the whole thing, telling myself to look away. There's no way he wants anyone to see him like this.

"Bailey," a voice barks.

"Sir?" I turn to Coach.

"I need you to get in there and take a knee, son."

"Yes, sir."

I almost fall the first step I take. The stumble jars me out of my daze.

"Let's go, Jordan!"

I try to find the voice in the crowd.

It's my mom's voice—I know that. But I can't spot her. After all, everyone's standing, applauding. At first I think they're applauding me, and maybe some of them are. But most of them are applauding Curt. They've probably been clapping for him since he began hobbling off the field. I was just too horrified to notice.

Now that he's on the sideline, most of the fans sit down except for Lance, who's actually grinning at me and yelling, "Streak! Streak! Streak!" It's gross, frankly. Grosser than the muck I'm standing in.

I finally spot my mom. She's standing too.

"You can do it, Jordan!" she shouts.

She doesn't look happy, though. She looks determined.

I look at Curt limping off.

"Bailey!" Coach barks. "What are you waiting for?"

I turn back to the field.

We don't bother to huddle up because everyone knows what to do.

Both sides line up.

I crouch under center and say, "Hike!"

The snap goes right through my hands and falls to the ground. I dive for the football. When I look up, though, I see that no one's lunging at me. Both sides just stand there, waiting for me to recover the football so the referees can blow their whistles and the game can finally end.

Chapter 14

It's Monday and they're chanting again in the cafeteria. I had been avoiding the cafeteria—facing the whole school—for as long as possible, until I couldn't walk around the hallway any longer. I tried to be as inconspicuous as possible, but as I slipped in the back Lance spotted me and started chanting.

Only this time it's not just about me.

"Curt's hurt! Time to streak! Curt's hurt! Time to streak!"

As usual, Lance bounds up and climbs on the table, leading the chants. People around him start joining in.

"Curt's hurt! Time to streak!"

How does Lance do it? How does he make people feel okay acting this way?

"Curt's hurt! Time to streak!"

His smile is as big now as it was on Friday after Curt needed help off the field. He turns to me beaming, like he expects me to be proud. But just like the last time he started the chanting in the cafeteria, my stomach is in knots. Just like last time I know what he wants me to do. Only now I'm not going to stick around for the rest of what I know is coming.

I turn and walk out of the room.

"Streak! Yo, Jordan. Slow down, dude."

I don't stop walking until Lance catches up to me and clamps a giant hand on my shoulder.

"Where you going, dude?" he asks, a little out of breath from running across the cafeteria to chase after me.

"As far away from there as possible," I say gesturing to the lunch room.

"We're just having some fun, dude."

"How is that fun? Huh? Believe it or

not, Curt is a human being. You know, with feelings and stuff? Have you heard of those?"

I think about Curt's grimacing face as he hobbled off the field.

"Relax, Bailey. Dang, dude—why are you protecting that guy? I mean, he's not even here today."

"He's not?" I ask.

"I may be a jerk," Lance says, as though he's proud of it, "but I'm not *that* much of a jerk."

"Why isn't Curt here?" I ask.

Lunch must be over. I can hear the sound of hundreds of feet entering the hallways.

"How should I know?" Lance says. "Probably still recovering or something."

"Or maybe he doesn't want to have to face this place. Could you blame him?"

"No," Lance says. "I've made it pretty rough for him." Maybe it's Lance's honesty that people find so appealing. He's always himself; I'll give Lance that. A showboating, trash-talking man of the people. "Then again," he continues, "Curt made it rough on himself too. I mean, all he had to do was play better or step aside. Or tell me to shut up. He was the quarterback of the team—it's not like he didn't have any power."

"I thought this was about me, not him," I say.

"It is, dude."

Students stream by us on their way to class. They clap both of our shoulders as they walk by. They tell me good luck and that they can't wait for Friday.

"I don't want to have any part of this," I tell Lance.

Lance calls after me as I walk away. "Don't worry about it, Streak. You just go to practice. I'll take care of everything else."

Chapter 15

The reporter and the cameraperson are nowhere to be found at practice.

Lance is there, though.

I watch him hop the fence and cross the field. It's not until he's thirty yards away that I realize he's talking to someone—himself? No, he's on his cell phone.

When he's only a few feet away he lifts the phone from his ear and says to me, "They seem to think the story's over." He shakes his head, baffled. "Don't worry, though"—he punches my shoulder pad reassuringly—"I got this."

"They just need to realize that the story's only just begun," he says to both me and whoever is on the other end of the phone call.

I have no doubt he's right. Knowing Lance, he'll probably talk the news station into bringing a camera for tomorrow's practice and every other practice I ever play in.

But I still can't help feeling relieved.

After all, this is my first practice as the starting quarterback.

I'll have plenty to worry about without having the practice recorded.

Chapter 16

"**H**ow was practice?" Mom asks.

We're sitting at the dinner table, waiting for Dad to put the finishing touches on whatever he's making.

"Fine," I say.

This is, surprisingly, the truth. I'd been silently dreading the possibility of this day, my first practice as a starting quarterback, ever since I made my amazing pass. But it didn't end up being so bad. Today, like every Monday, was a running and defense day. That meant my only job was to take the snap and hand the ball to our running backs. On option plays I pitched the ball to the running back every time, even when I probably should have run with it myself. For whatever reason, Coach didn't seem to mind. Actually, he didn't seem to mind much of anything. When players jumped offside or made some other mistake, he made us all run—just like he always does. But he didn't scream at the player or lecture all of us about discipline and the importance of getting the little things right. At the end of practice Lando asked him how Curt was doing. Coach just grunted, "Broken leg" and then got back to talking about East Elm, our next opponent. It was a quiet, sad practice that lacked the usual energy Coach demands from us. But I also didn't get smeared into the ground like I thought I would.

"Oh, c'mon," Mom says. "Your lifelong dream is about to come true, and all you can say is that things are fine?"

"It's a lot to take in," I say.

"If it's too much to take in," Dad says from across the kitchen, "you could always change your mind about playing Glorified Violence Ball—I mean football."

Ever since he caved about letting me play football, he's been jokingly trying to talk me out of it. Of course, Mom and I know that he's not really joking—that he'd love it if I reconsidered playing. But, of course, he doesn't know that I've wanted to take him up on the offer pretty much since he started making it.

"Not on your life, Steve," Mom says. Clearly, she's not in a joking mood. "This Friday I get to go see my son be the starting quarterback, a position he earned through his talent and determination."

She smiles at me and squeezes my elbow.

"I'm not so sure I earned it," I say.

"Is that what this mood of yours is about? Do you feel guilty about Curt's injury? It's not your fault, Jordan, if that's what you're thinking."

"Why would it be my fault?"

It had never occurred to me that I should take the blame for Curt's injury. I mean . . . what?

"Exactly," Mom says. "It's not."

"Then why'd you bring it up?"

"Sorry. It's just, the way Curt got injured—I was worried you thought he didn't take a knee at the end of the game because he was trying to prove something to all your fans who thought he shouldn't be the starter. You moped around the house all weekend, and that's the only explanation I could come up with." She squints her eyes and sighs. "Glad I was wrong."

The thing is, she's not wrong. I hadn't been thinking about any of this until right now, but I should have been. Curt got injured—he broke his leg!—because fans were booing him over and over all because of me. Until he decided to prove them wrong. That's when the trouble happened.

I *am* partly to blame for what happened to him.

"Dinner is served," Dad says, placing a large plate of chicken and a bowl of rice on the table. He tells us what the meal is called: chicken followed by some word I've never heard.

"Are you coming to the game, Dad?"

"No promises," he says. "But I'll try, okay?"

Which we both know is just his way of saying no.

"I'll be there, Jordan," Mom says.

"Thanks, Jordan," I reply, trying to muster a smile.

Chapter

17

Lance keeps telling me the news crew will show up to the next practice. But they don't.

They're not here on Tuesday, Wednesday, or Thursday. Apparently they're convinced the story is over. Frankly, I get where they're coming from. After all, the Coach's kid is now hurt, so there's no longer a quarterback controversy.

Speaking of Curt—he's not at practice either.

I mean, I know he broke his leg, but it's still strange not to see him at practice. No matter how much he had to put up with from Lance and the others, the next day he'd be right back on the field, his stocky legs planted firmly to the ground. No amount of yelling was going to budge Curt Cole an inch.

As for Coach Cole? He's at practice each day, but just barely. His body's there, but his mind is somewhere else. There's no blood boiling in his cheeks.

The worst part of the week is Wednesday. That's when I'm supposed to drop back and throw some passes. But unlike Tuesday, this is a full-contact practice. My adrenaline is pumping so hard I can barely hear myself say, "Hut!" Then, when I drop back, the same thing happens to me that happened last year. Everything goes blurry. I move my head from side to side, trying to get my vision to snap back. Trying to find an open receiver. But all I can see is frantic motion. I stand there and stand there for what feels like forever. Then Kevin Rock, our all-conference linebacker, smashes me to the ground. I think it's was Kevin who helps me up, but it isn't. It's Coach.

"You okay, son?" he asks, under his breath.

"Yes, sir," I say, but I think the way my

voice and body are still shaking gives me away. That's when he announces that from here on out every practice this week will be non-contact. "We don't need any more injuries," he explains to the team. "We're undefeated. Let's stay that way."

Knowing I'm not going to get blasted helps me clear my head. For the next few days I throw the ball well and—just as importantly—I execute all the plays. My main goal is to run the plays exactly like Curt used to.

It isn't just a clear head that motivates me. It's guilt.

After Thursday's practice, I wait until my teammates leave the locker room. Then I tap on Coach's office door.

He makes a grunting sound that I'm pretty sure means "Come in."

"Coach?" I say. "I mean, sir?"

"What is it, son?" he replies.

"It's . . . it's . . ." I stammer.

"Spit it out, Bailey."

"I'm sorry," I finally manage.

"Eh?" he grunts.

"I'm sorry if I had anything to do with Curt's injury, Coach. I know he should have taken a knee—that was the right thing to do—and Curt usually does the right thing—and the only reason I can think of that he didn't do the right thing was—"

"Save it, Bailey," Coach interrupts. The words themselves are harsh, but his tone isn't. "All that stuff, you can't bring it on the field with you tomorrow. We need you focused. We need you ready. The present moment. That's all that matters. Set the other stuff aside."

I bet he's been telling himself the same thing all week. It's good advice, but it's easier said than done. Coach hasn't exactly been focused on the present moment lately. And if he can't do it, how can I?

"Is that it, Bailey?" he asks.

"Yes, sir."

***

When I get out of the locker room, I see Lance. He's taping another poster on the wall.

Over the last few days he's single-handedly covered the school with them. Some are simple. They say STREAK! or OPERATION! AERIAL ASSAULT! (Launch Date: this FRIDAY!) Others look like giant trading cards. One poster has the front of the card: an action shot of me playing quarterback at practice. The poster next to it has the back of the card. It includes my height, weight, position ("Future All-Time Great QB"), throwing arm, etc. It even has made-up amazing stats (56 TDs, 0 INTs, etc.).

The poster Lance is currently putting up says TODAY'S THE DAY HISTORY IS MADE! "The game's tomorrow," I say.

Lance pivots around. "Right. But no one's going to see this until tomorrow."

"Good point," I say.

"You sound tired, dude." Lance fishes his phone out of his pocket. "This will cheer you up." He tilts the phone on its side to make the image fill the whole screen. We watch a YouTube video of me throwing passes at practice. "I edited out all the incompletions," Lance says.

I mumble a reply, but my heart's not in it.

"Man, you really are tired. That's what happens when you're not used to getting all the snaps."

"Yeah."

"Rest up, dude," Lance says. "You just worry about putting on a show during the game. I'll put on a show everywhere else."

I turn for the parking lot, then stop. "Hey, Lance?"

"Yeah, dude?"

"Why do you care so much? About me playing, I mean?"

Lance doesn't hesitate. "Because it's right," he says. "Because Coach has to know what he's done is wrong. Because this is how things are supposed to be. People with your talent are supposed to walk around like kings in high school."

I don't ask him any more questions, because we both know what he means.

People like me are people like *Lance*.

This isn't just a chance to settle a score for him. It's a chance to make the world make sense again. Lance was supposed to be the star player. He was supposed to be the one walking around like a king. If he can't rule the school, at least he can name his successor.

"You're already a legend, dude," he says. "All you have to do now is play like it."

Chapter 18

Lance has always been good at getting the fans riled up. But this week he's outdone himself. It's still twenty minutes before game time, but the chants are already deafening.

"STREAK! STREAK! STREAK!"

They get even louder every time I throw a pass during warm-ups.

Part of me thinks Curt's lucky. Why couldn't I have been the one to break my leg? I know it is a terrible thing to wish for, but honestly, how am I supposed to live up to these people's expectations?

Coach Cole does his best to ease me into the game. On the first series, he calls three run plays. We punt it back to East Elm amid a chorus of boos.

The next series is the same: three run plays and a punt.

"Let Streak loose! Let Streak loose!" the fans scream.

There's no doubt Lance is behind the new chant.

But Coach doesn't let me loose. Not the next series, or the series after that. We just keep running. We manage to get one first down, but other than that our offense is useless. East Elm loads the box on every play, bringing extra players to clog the running lanes. They're leaving themselves vulnerable to the pass, but only if we, well, pass.

And Coach has no interest in doing that.

It's not that he's stubborn. It's that he's tough. He's willing to take the blame for *my* fears. *My* cowardice.

By the end of the half, we're down 7–0 and I still haven't attempted a pass.

The crowd looks like it's about to riot. Some parents are actually cussing Coach Cole out. They've come here to see Jordan Bailey Jr., myth, legend, and YouTube sensation. (Today in school Lance showed me that the highlight video he made for me has over 20,000 hits.)

But instead of Aaron Rodgers 2.0 hurling the ball all over the field, all they've gotten to see is bodies piled at the line of scrimmage.

Somebody throws their hot chocolate at Coach as we jog into the locker room at the half. He's still dripping when Tom Mortenson, one of our defensive backs, mutters under his breath: "Maybe a pass would be good."

"What's that, Mortenson?" Coach snaps.

"Nothing, sir."

We're in the locker room, sitting on the benches. I think it's going to end there, but then Ahmed Bari, our defensive end, speaks up. "We're working our butts off on defense, Coach. It'd be nice to get some help."

I look around the room at the rest of our defense. Every one of them is breathing loudly. They look completely gassed.

"Working your butts off, eh?" Coach says. "According to the scoreboard you've given up seven points to a mediocre team." For the first time all week, his face turns its normal shade of red. He sighs. "Look—I get it. Too much is being asked of you. But the truth is, I don't know what to do about that. This is Bailey's first time starting. Remember what that felt like for you? Remember how nervous you were?" He's looking at Ahmed, but I know the message is for everyone. "You were lucky, though. Your job was to hit people. Getting rid of your nerves was easy. Now imagine your first game was at quarterback. And everyone in the stands thinks you're a walking legend." He looks to me. "No offense, Bailey, but you're not a walking legend."

"None taken, sir," I say.

"No offense again, Bailey, but I for one am afraid you're going to screw up and jeopardize our perfect season."

I actually smile. It's like he's reading my mind.

"Yes, sir," I say.

"So as long as we're only down a touchdown, my suggestion is we open more holes for our running backs and force more turnovers on defense. That okay with all of you?"

I'm not sure it *is* okay with everyone else. Some of them have probably been hoping I'd get to start all season. They've bought into Lance's hype. But they also know this isn't really an invitation to give feedback.

"Yes, sir," they mumble.

***

We get pummeled with more boos on our way back to the field.

Coach is right, though. So long as we're within a touchdown, there's no reason to try a risky pass play. After all, we may have a lot of great athletes on defense, but even if I weren't a terrified coward, I wouldn't have anyone to throw to. When he got the job, Coach decided to play a conservative brand of offense, which meant that none of the good athletes went out for wide receiver.

As long as our defense is in pouncing range, the best strategy is to protect the football and hope East Elm doesn't.

In the middle of the third quarter, we're on offense. We've got the ball deep in our own territory. I hand the ball off to our running back, Ben Lester, who charges across the line of scrimmage. I can't see what happens next. It could be a hand or a helmet that pops the football out of Ben's arm. However it happens, I see the ball in the air, and I see an East Elm player grab it and go to the ground.

Their offense now has the ball at our three yard line and four chances to score another touchdown.

It takes them all four, but they do it.

The score: East Elm 14, Clover Ridge 0.

"Bailey!" Coach says. "Listen up. I need to call some pass plays, but I'm not doing it because of them."

He's referring to the fans. Some of them are still yelling, "Let Streak Loose!" Some are yelling much worse.

"This is the right football decision. I need you—*we* need you—to throw the ball. Okay?"

"Okay, sir," I say.

"You've got a great arm, son," he says. "Now's the time to show it."

"I'll try, sir."

And that's exactly what I do. Try.

But as soon as I take the snap, everything goes blurry again. My heart beat is a snare drum. The only thing I can make out are the bodies scrambling to tackle me.

I tell myself to focus, but before I get a chance to do that I'm on my back with a giant East Elm player lying on top of me.

Coach calls another pass play, but when I look downfield everything's a jumble.

How can I throw if I can't even pick out the receivers?

This is what I'm thinking as I lie on my back again and wait for a teammate to help me up.

The same thing happens on third down.

It's not the offensive line's fault. They're giving me plenty of time to throw. I'm just too scared? Or overwhelmed? Or . . . something.

No matter how hard I try, I can't get my body to cooperate. My eyes won't work. My arm won't budge.

I stand like a statue until I'm finally toppled, over and over, by East Elm players.

By the fourth quarter Coach has called several more pass plays, but I haven't thrown the ball once.

The crowd has gone from chanting my name to total silence. They might as well be watching my funeral.

Except I'm not dead. Not yet.

"Hut!" I say once more, backpedaling with the football. By now East Elm's expecting a pass. Their linemen have their ears pinned back. They're in attack mode. I barely have enough time to bring the ball to my ear before two of them collide into me from behind.

From the bottom of a pile of bodies, I look at the sideline and for the first time realize Curt's there. He's staring right at me. Fiercely.

He looks angry. The hand that isn't holding a crutch is closed in a fist.

No, not angry, I think. *Determined.*

It makes me feel determined too.

Here I am, crunched under a pile of huge bodies.

But somehow, I'm still okay.

For over a quarter I've been crushed and creamed. I've been smacked and smeared.

But I'm still mostly fine.

Sore, beaten up—but fine.

All my limbs are intact. I can breathe and blink. Rather than being blinded by adrenaline, I'm now riding high on it.

For the first time since my first game, I realize, I'm no longer scared.

***

It's late in the game now—less than a minute to go—and Coach Cole suggests we run the ball.

"I can do this, Coach," I tell him. "Give me another chance."

"There's nothing to do, Bailey. The

game's out of reach. I'm sorry I put you in this position, son, but—"

"I can do this," I repeat. "Please. I need to do this, Coach." I look at him and then at Curt, standing next to him.

Back to Coach. He squints at me and finally nods.

This time, for the first time, my head and eyes are clear as I drop back. I can see each of my receivers, lumbering down the field. Part of me is conscious of the pocket collapsing around me, but I ignore this part. After all, what's the worst East Elm can do to me?

It's as if everything is suddenly in slow-motion.

Actually, it sort of is. My receivers aren't exactly fast runners.

I wait for them to get open. I wait some more.

None of them have any separation from their defenders, but I decide to throw anyway.

Eddie Eagon's running a post route, one of my favorites. I give the ball some arc, hoping to get it over the top of the defender. It's a good throw. If he were open, it would have hit him in stride.

But he's not open.

The East Elm corner back gets to the football first and picks it off.

The crowd breaks its silence in a deafening roar.

"BOO!" they yell. "BOOOOOOOO!"

This time it's not Coach they're booing. It's me.

And I've never felt so good in my life. For once they see me for who I am. And I'm okay with that.

Chapter 19

I'm still feeling good as I get in my car to drive home. For a full year I've had this big secret. I'm not worthy of their hype. I've kept the secret because I was afraid of disappointing everyone.

But now that I *have* disappointed everyone, all I feel is relief.

I'm glad they know. Coach asked me to try, and that's exactly what I did.

Tried. And failed.

With everyone watching.

The fans have every right to be disappointed. The perfect season is gone, and so is the myth that Lance created. But me? This is the first time I can honestly say I'm not disappointed in myself.

***

It's late when I finally park in our driveway. The TV is on but muted in the living room.

I'm not surprised to see my mom sleeping on the couch.

I *am* surprised to see my dad on the couch too.

Unlike Mom, he's awake.

He gets up as quietly as possible. "Follow me to the kitchen," he whispers. "I'll warm up some pork chops for you."

I take a seat at the kitchen table. In a voice just above a whisper, I say, "Sorry I'm so late. Did Mom tell you the game didn't go so hot?"

"She didn't have to tell me," Dad says, futzing with the oven. "I was there."

"You were?"

"Your mother practically picked me up and threw me in the car."

"Then you know you were right."

Dad looks up from the oven. "About what?"

"Football being violent or whatever."

"Of course football's violent, Jordan. Everyone knows that. But you're still in one piece, aren't you?"

I look down at my body. My legs are aching and I can already feel bruises developing all over from the sacks I took.

"Can I ask you something?" Dad says. He opens a cabinet, pulls out a cooking tray.

"Sure," I reply, not sure what he's going to say.

"Why did you decide to throw that last pass? You hadn't gotten the ball out of your hand all night, then all of a sudden you did."

"I don't know. I guess it didn't really matter anymore. I could have done anything and the result would have been the same. I just," I hesitate, unsure if I should tell him the truth or keep up the charade. "I just wanted to see if I *could*, you know?"

Dad nods, opens the oven door, and we stand there in silence for a little while.

"At first," Dad suddenly cuts in, "when I saw you getting knocked down on the field tonight, I was worried about you. But then it kept happening, and to my surprise I felt something else."

I watch him ladle the sauce and waited for him to continue.

"Pride," he says. "There you were, getting back up again. Running on and off the field. I don't care if you play football or not, Jordan. What I care about is you—and nothing's going to change that."

"I don't care if you play football, either," a voice says.

It's Mom. She had made her way over from the couch as Dad and I were talking.

"You know that, right? After tonight," she says, "I totally understand if you never want to see a football field again."

"Actually," I tell her, "I can't wait to get back on the field." For the first time in a while, I'm not lying to them or anyone else about football.

Chapter 20

Before I get back to the football field, though, I have two stops to make.

The first is school.

It's Saturday, so I'm worried the school will be locked up. Luckily, a teacher or a janitor must be working today, because the front door is open. When I get inside, I head straight for a wall.

There's one reason and one reason only that I'm here. I grab one of the *STREAK!* posters and tear it off the wall. Then I grab another, and another. The plan is to keep tearing until the walls are bare.

"Good idea, dude."

Lance is twenty feet away from me. I texted him earlier this morning and told him to meet me here.

"We need to come up with a brand-new campaign. Maybe something about you making an epic comeback. People love comeback stories." The words are typical Lance. But they lack his usual vigor. He sounds more sincere than I've heard him be in a long time.

"I don't think even *you* could sell that story, Lance."

He thinks about it, nods. "You're probably right. Can I ask you something?"

I tear off another poster. "Sure."

"You never wanted to be a star, did you?"

"Not really," I admit.

"That's what I thought. Not sure how I missed that all this time."

"Not your fault," I say, ripping away another poster. "I didn't tell you."

"Why not?"

"Because you quit the team for me, Lance. I didn't want you to think it was all for nothing."

Lance doesn't say anything for a while. The only sound is me tearing up posters.

"I didn't quit, dude."

I let go of a poster and turn around.

"What?" I ask him.

"I didn't quit. Coach Cole kicked me off the team. I went into his office and demanded that he start you over Curt. He said he'd had enough of me—that no player is bigger than the team."

"Why'd you say you quit?"

"I was too ashamed, dude. Saying I'd boycotted the team sounded way better than admitting I was kicked to the curb. What I could never figure out is why Coach Cole never corrected my story."

"He's weird like that," I agree.

We don't say anything else because there doesn't seem to be anything left to say.

Lance steps up to the wall. Together the two of us remove all traces of the Jordan Bailey that Lance spent the last year creating.

Chapter 21

The two of us arrive at Coach Cole's house later that afternoon. When Coach opens the door, I half expect him to slam the door in our faces—or at least Lance's.

But he just nods at us and opens the door wider so we can step inside. Even at home he's wearing his Clover Ridge hat. Is he ever not a coach?

"I'm actually here to see Curt," I say.

Coach points me in the right direction.

As I walk through the house, I hear Lance awkwardly start talking to Coach. "I'm sorry, sir. I honestly don't know what else to say."

I'm really not sure Lance totally gets how awfully he's behaved, but it's a good start, at the very least.

I reach the living room and find Curt lying in front of the TV, crutches on the floor beside the couch. His left foot is propped on the couch's armrest. It's covered to the knee in a cast.

It's amazing, though. Even lying down like this, he still looks powerful. His square body takes up every inch of the couch, sturdy even with the cast.

I should probably say hi first, maybe talk about the weather. But I launch right into the reason I'm here. "It's my fault you're in that cast."

Curt takes his eyes off whatever show he's watching. "What?"

"Your leg. It's my fault. And I'm—"

"How do you figure?" he says. "Did you make the mud extra sticky?"

"No. I—"

"Did you give me milk with reduced calcium, thus allowing my bones to weaken?"

"Huh? No, what I'm—"

"Did you scramble my brains while I was sleeping so I'd make stupid decisions?"

Honestly, this guy doesn't pull any punches. This is the second time I've tried to be nice to him, and it's the second time that he's snapped at me.

"I let people treat you horribly," I say, "and you tried to prove them wrong, and now here you are—"

"Exactly," Curt interrupts, "*I* tried to prove them wrong. I didn't just get on a knee and run out the clock. And now *I* can't run out of *anything*. This is my fault, and I can live with that. What I can't live with is your weak apology."

"Okay," I say. "Sorry I brought it up. I mean—you know what I mean. I'll get out of here, okay?"

I back out of the room.

"Thanks, though," Curt says. "For the weak apology, I mean. I don't accept it, but thanks anyway."

I'm 99 percent sure he's being sincere, so I step back into the living room.

"So you had a rough time last night," Curt says.

"That's an understatement," I reply.

"That's because you tried to play like me. You can't do that."

"I noticed."

"No, I mean, I'm good at keeping the team on the field. Bulldozing my way through the line. If the team needs four yards, I can get us four yards. If the team needs twenty yards, I can get us four yards." He smiles. "You know what I mean? I'm good at getting first downs, keeping the offense on the field, letting our defense rest. Touchdowns? That I'm not so good at. You may have noticed my pathetic arm."

I don't say anything. It's one thing for an injured guy to make fun of himself. It's another thing for you to make fun of him.

"You should have played your game, man," Curt says.

"I tried that. It didn't work very well, either."

"That's because you didn't have anyone to throw to."

"It was more than that," I admit, "but that definitely didn't help."

"You need that low-life scumbag right there." He picks up his crutch and points above me.

I look over my shoulder. Sure enough, Lance is standing behind me. He steps into the living room.

"That's what I was thinking too," I say. "But only if it's okay with you and your dad."

He doesn't make eye contact with Lance. "Personally," Curt says, "I hate Lance Brockman."

"Fair enough," Lance agrees.

Curt still doesn't acknowledge his presence. "I hate him more than just about anything I can think of. In fact, there's only one thing in the world I hate more than Lance Brockman. Losing. We lost last night, and the thought of that hurts me almost as much as my leg. So if you're saying he can help us win, then my answer is yes. Let him back on the team."

Curt still hasn't made any eye contact with Lance. In fact, he's not even looking at me anymore.

"You sure?" a voice booms from behind us.

I hadn't notice Coach enter the room.

"Just don't expect me to stop hating him," Curt says. "I've been pretending he doesn't exist for over a year now, and I don't plan to stop anytime soon."

"Thanks, dude," Lance says, and I can tell he's truly grateful. He even reaches one of his giant hands toward Curt's shoulder, then thinks better of it.

Which is probably for the best. Curt's still holding a crutch, and my guess is he's not afraid to use it.

Chapter

22

"What do you got for us, Bailey?" Lando asks.

We're huddled up, trying to catch our breath. It's third and a long eight yards. Fourth quarter. It's been a month since we lost to East Elm. In that time, we've gotten better and better. Well, okay, I've gotten better and better. The rest of the team was already really good.

This is the sectional finals. Whoever wins this game goes to the state tournament.

I look at Lance. "Streak?"

By now Coach has enough confidence in me that I'm allowed to call my own plays.

To my surprise, Lance shakes his head. "We don't need that yet. Besides, it's what they're expecting. They've got two deep in the zone."

They is North Rapids, and the reason they're expecting it is because we've already gone deep. Twice.

"Pitch it on my side to Lester," Lance says. "I'll do the rest."

I look around the huddle to make sure we're all on the same page.

"Ready," I say.

"Break!" we shout in unison.

I walk up to the line, looking to my left and then my right.

We need to convert this third down. We're up by three, but if we have to punt North Rapids will get the ball back with plenty of time on the clock.

I take a deep breath, slow my heartbeat, try to take everything in.

Instead of the world going fuzzy like it used to, it becomes clearer. Now I can see that Lance is right. North Rapids has two players dropped way back to protect against the long pass.

I notice the stuff going on off the field too.

This is an away game, but our fans came out in droves.

"Clover Ridge!" they shout. "Clover Ridge!"

I can't see them, but I know that two of the people shouting are my parents.

Curt is up there somewhere too. Instead of standing on the sideline, he's decided to crutch his way up the steps. Up there, he says, he can do a better job analyzing the game. He's got a walkie talkie that he uses to communicate directly with Coach Cole.

This one's for you, Curt, I think to myself.

Curt said before that I couldn't play quarterback like he does, and he was right. But in this case I'm going to do my best impression.

I crouch down under center, say, "Hike!"

I get the snap cleanly, pivot, and pitch the ball to Ben Lester. He takes off running to the outside.

It's not part of the play, but I follow him. It's what Curt would have done. I lower my shoulder and slam it into a North Rapids player. We both fall to the ground, but I scramble to my feet and run after the play.

Ben gets the eight yards we needed and is still on the loose.

Ahead of him, Lance tramples the cornerback and the free safety. I catch up to Lance just as Ben crosses into the end zone.

Check out all
the GRIDIRON Books

Leave it all on the field!

Check out all the titles in the

bOUNCE

Collection

STEP UP YOUR GAME

Paul Hoblin lives, teaches, and writes in Saint Paul, Minnesota.